D0517598

A Special Thanks!

This book is a testament to the power of community and love, and would not
have been possible without so many wonderful family and friends.
I have been so blessed in my life to have such an
amazing community around me, and it was through your
generosity and support that this book exists today!

Though I wish I could list every single person
that has supported me, there is a small group of individuals that were
extremely generous with their contributions to my campaign.
Thank you all again for believing in me!

Travis Jaeger & Michelle Souleret

Martha & Rob Silk

Steve & Mary Frances Silk Eshleman

Lynn Yates

For all those who have been there since the beginning
and new friends who have joined us along the way,
thank you for Joining the Adventure,
and Completing the Adventure!

The Lost Castle

Black Water Bog

Great Willow Tree

Great Sea of Grass

RJ the Mouse took a stroll through the woods,
He came to a point where a crossroad stood.
From the path less traveled he heard a cry,
"Should I help today, or just pass by?"

Making the right choice can be hard, it's true,
But RJ knew the right thing to do.
A gentle hush fell in the woods,
He felt a presence guide him to where a small house stood.

The path was a maze
and RJ its guest,

"Who is this presence,
and why is it not at rest?"

He felt the past had come to stay,

RJ didn't know why

and he could not say,

The moment was broken by a gentle voice,

"Go away song
that is my choice!"

He opened the door, letting in the fresh air,

An elderly hedgehog said, "Hello there."

She was small and cute with red rosy cheeks,

Her quills were round and scraped the ground at her feet.

Her gaze was soft and with a tear in her eye,

She asked, "Is that you singing that beautiful lullaby?"

RJ listened, "I'm sorry no..."

"My name is RJ,
an adventuring mouse."

"My name is Tek
- welcome to my house."

"Sometimes at night I sing
songs with my mother."

"You two are very blessed
to still have each other."

Tek gazed at the sun, the woods, and the hill,
Lost in her thoughts, somewhere time stands still.

"I have an idea," said RJ.
"Sing me the song you are hearing today.
A tangled thought is a frustrating thing,
And an untangling adventure is just what I can bring!"

"I suppose we could, why it is a lovely eve.
But you must stay with me and promise not to leave."

"The world is big with many stories to discover,
Like ones with lost castles, owls, and others.
But now it will be your adventure we uncover!"

RJ said, "Remember, be strong." Tek smiled, beginning the song:

"From memories old, there's a love that will last.
Together we walk through the Great Sea of Grass,
Close your eyes, and do not cry.
A love that's true from memories past."

Gathering their things they began on their way,
Ready to follow the beautiful song on this day.

The Great Sea of Grass was a sight to behold,
It stretched to the horizon and was very old.
The golden sun set low in the sky,
The grass gently waved and looked alive.

Tek gazed at the grass, the sky, and the land,
"I remember this place," She said, squeezing RJ's hand.
"The breeze and the love, it's the little things in life,
When they come together and make a moment right."

RJ said, "Remember, be strong."
Tek smiled, and began the next verse of the song:

"Soaring above from a distant height,
Shining through the Whispering Willows at night.
No need to fear, my presence is clear;
A silent guardian in the moon's light."

The Whispering Willows and their tender tune,
Gently swayed under the newly lit moon.
They followed the trail and the path that lay bare,
The moon was their guide in the mid summer's air.

Tek stood quietly on the trail in the wood,
"I feel someone with me," she said, putting up her hood.
"It's familiar and strange, but peaceful and true,
Like an intimate love that I barely knew."

RJ said, "Remember, be strong."
Tek smiled, and began the next verse of the song:

"A nocturnal chorus sings our song
In the Isle Woods walking all night long.
No words to speak at the summer's peak;
A gentle song to connect us when I'm gone."

The Isle Woods were ancient and old,
Their stories from the past are often told.
With crickets that sing bygone songs,
Guiding the brave who journey along.

Tek heard their song and became very sad,
"Something about this place makes me feel bad.
This life of mine – I can't remember the start,
But something is telling me to find the voice in my heart."

RJ said, "Remember, be strong."
Tek smiled, and began the next verse of the song:

"Live for the moments that are tender and mild.
Etched in time on the Tree that is Wild,
A promise in moonlight, on that gentle night.
Forever and ever my sweet child."

On the edge of the night rose the Tree that is Wild,
A golden oak, a guardian that was gentle and mild.
A friend of the land, the moon, and the sky,
Its ancient branches waved at those who passed by.

RJ walked Tek to the base of the tree,
But stood back as this was her destiny.
It is said what is lost is never truly gone,
A heart etched in the tree said,

"Love Forever, Tek & Mom."

Tek traced her fingers in the carving on the tree,

"Mom? That's been you this whole time with me?
I remember your voice now and its sweet sound,
You were taken from me and never found.
It's been so long, I can hardly remember your face!"
A whisper in the wind gently said, "Then give me a chase!"

And just like that the song departed,
"Follow that voice!" The chase had now started!

Together they waved to the ancient oak tree,
Chasing the song down the trail as fast as could be!

The night was still dark despite the full moon,
RJ cut a path giving chase to the tune.
In and out the song faded away,
It danced in the night now leading the way.
The chorus of the Isle Woods sang in the moonlight,
"Follow that good song into the night!"

Onwards they went as quick as they could,
They flew like birds moving faster than they should.
They shattered the waves of the gentle grass,
Leaving a great ripple in the night as they passed.
Faster they chased and now weary in their bones,
The song was almost lost when they ended at Tek's home!

RJ collapsed and Tek fell to her knees,

"Mom are you here? Sing to me please!"

The night was silent and a light rain started to fall.

There was nothing to hear, not anything at all...

The song appeared lost in the dark night,
But all hope was not lost, no not tonight!
From the woods a gentle figure appeared,
It said, "Come to me, my little dear."

"I thought I lost you,
I thought you were gone?"
With a cry,
Tek ran to the arms of her mom!

"My little Tek, no,
I've been with you all along,"
Beautifully her mom sang
the forgotten verse of the song:

"A mother's love cannot be contained,

Though memories fade,

A heart remembers the love that was gained.

Our love unites, through dreams in the night.

When I held your hand and walked in the summer rain."

RJ stood proud with a tear in his eye,

A forgotten voice now found it was time to say goodbye.

He gave Tek a hug, "Now you're right where you belong."

She smiled, "Thank you again, and remember, be strong."

The Lost Castle

Black Water Bog

Great Willow Tree

Great Sea of Grass

Tree that is Wild

Isle Woods

- - - - - RJ's Journey

For Robert and Cassidy,
My Children,
My Inspiration

Never hesitate or be afraid to do what is right.
Stand with those who need guidance and light.
-Dad

I can't say thank you enough to Travis Jaeger and his continued support and guidance over the years!
Your insight is invaluable and I couldn't have done it without you!

Thank you again to my beautiful wife Katie for supporting me in this endeavor during a very difficult time in our lives.
Your love and support have meant so much to me,
and I cannot thank you enough from the bottom of my heart.
- Your Loving Husband

Made in the USA
San Bernardino, CA
01 March 2019

When RJ the Mouse hears a sad cry in the woods,
he has a choice to make, continue on his way,
or stop and help? A simple act of kindness can
change a life.

Armed with his courage, patience, and love RJ
helps Tek, an elderly hedgehog, on an adventure
that spans a lifetime.

He learns courage isn't always about heroic deeds,
but simple ones that put others first.

Together they set out, but will they discover the
forgotten voice in Tek's heart...

illustrated by Sophie Mitchell
edited by Travis Jaeger

ISBN 9781976837296

9 781976 837296